To:

From:

**"God gave the growth."**
**—1 Corinthians 3:6**

Visit us on the Web!
rhcbooks.com
BerenstainBears.com

Educators and librarians, for a variety of teaching tools, visit us at RHTeachersLibrarians.com

Library of Congress Control Number: 2021950870
ISBN 978-0-593-30252-1 (trade) — ISBN 978-0-593-30526-3 (ebook)

MANUFACTURED IN CHINA
10 9 8 7 6 5 4 3 2 1

# The Berenstain Bears
# Gifts of the Spirit
# Growing Up

**Mike Berenstain**

Based on the characters created by
Stan and Jan Berenstain

**Random House** 🏠 **New York**

Ever since Honey Bear was very little, she had loved her blue blankie. She slept with it when she was a baby. She cuddled with it in her crib. She rubbed it on her ear while she listened to bedtime stories.

Honey loved that snuggly blue blankie!

Honey still took her blankie with her everywhere. She ate with it. She dragged it around behind her when she played.

She wore it as a cape when she pretended she was Superbear!

The problem was, Honey's blankie was getting quite dirty.
Even worse, it was starting to smell!

Besides, Mama and Papa were beginning to feel that Honey was getting too old for a blankie. She couldn't drag it around with her forever! Perhaps it was time to help her grow up a bit and leave the blankie behind.

"We must do something about Honey's blankie," said Mama one day. "She's getting too old for it. And it's very dirty!"
"What can we do?" asked Papa.

"We could throw it in the trash," said Brother.

"We could throw it in the garbage," said Sister.

"We could burn it," said Papa.

"No," said Mama. "Honey Bear loves her blankie. That would break her heart! We need to help her grow out of it somehow."

"We'll have to do something," said Papa. "It's so dirty!"

"Hmm," said Mama. "I'll think about it."
And Mama did think about it. . . .

Mama thought about Honey's blankie while she was going about her daily routine. She thought about it while she dusted.

She thought about it as she vacuumed. She thought about it while she gardened and as she worked on one of her beautiful quilts.

That evening, Mama prayed about Honey's blankie. She even dreamed about Honey's blankie as she slept that night! All that thinking and praying and dreaming must have worked. When Mama woke up the next morning, she had a plan.

Mama waited until Honey's nap time. Then, as Honey slept, Mama carefully sneaked her blankie out from under her arm and put it in the washing machine.

It was thoroughly washed and came out sparkling clean. It wasn't dirty anymore, and it didn't smell bad either!

Carefully, Mama put the nice, clean blankie back under
Honey's arm. Sweet little Honey never even knew it was gone!

That evening, at dinner, the family noticed something different. Honey didn't have her blankie with her! She wasn't holding it. She wasn't dragging it around behind her. She wasn't wearing it as a cape. They were amazed!

"Where's your blankie, Honey?" Brother asked.

"Something happened to it," said Honey. "It smells funny now. So I gave it to Little Lady. I think I'm getting too grown-up for a blankie anyway."

The whole family let out a huge sigh of relief!

And everyone smiled as Little Lady happily chewed away on her nice, new, clean blankie!